Time to Go!

By Marta Cunill

Translated by Susan Ouriou

Owlkids Books

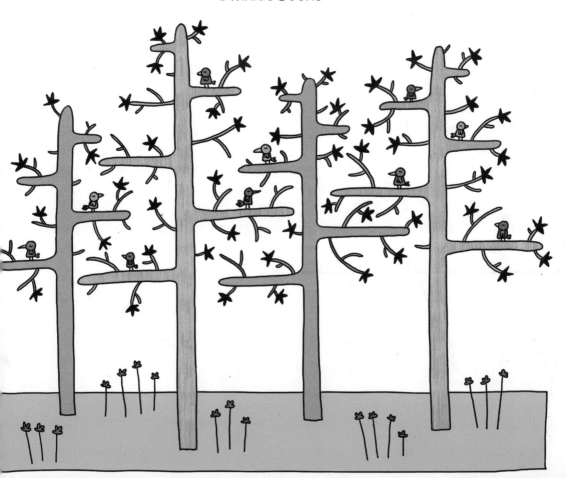

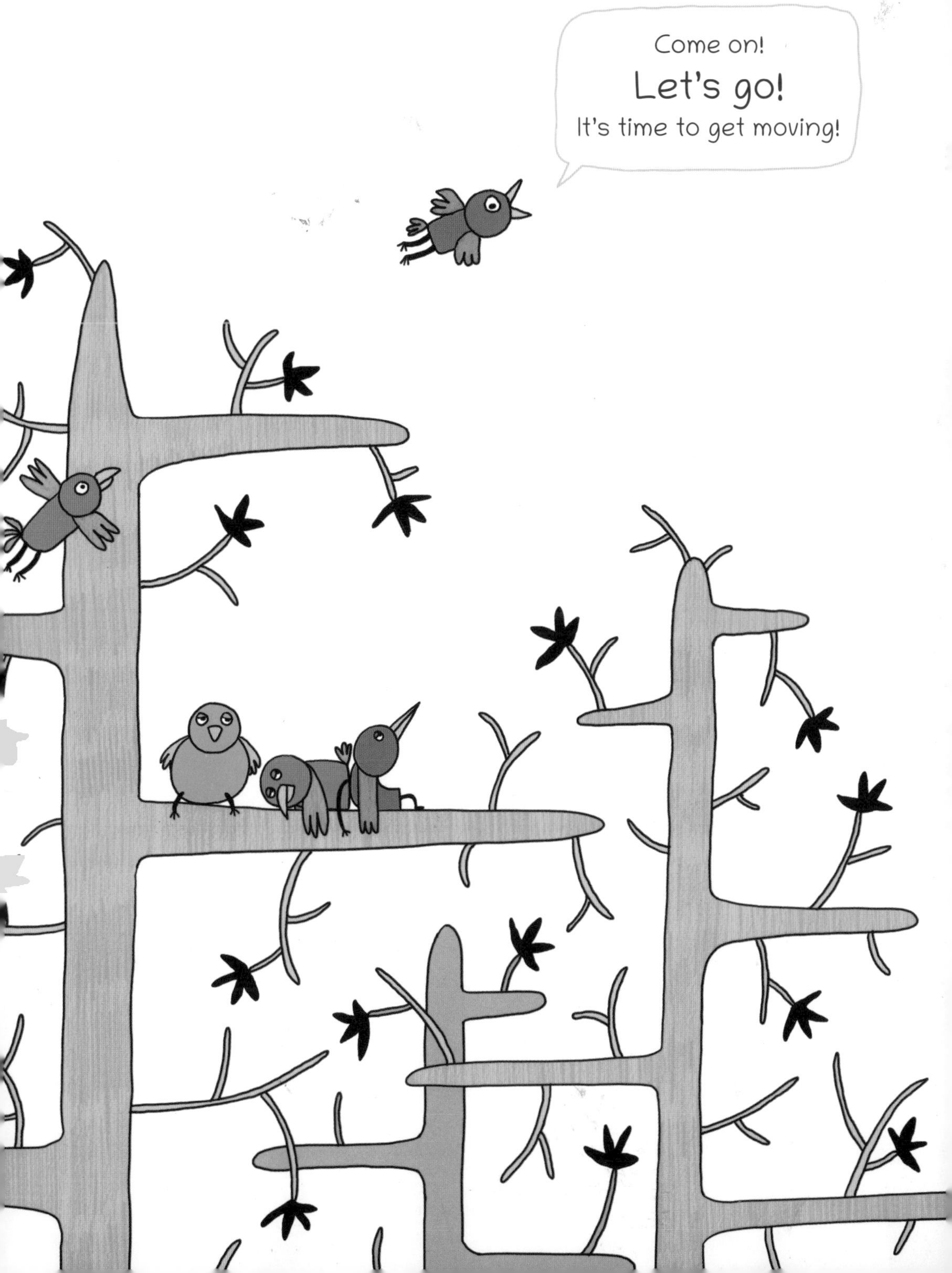
Come on!
Let's go!
It's time to get moving!

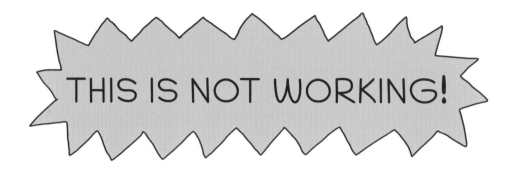

They find the other birds . . .

but they are a bit late.

Text and illustrations © 2018 Marta Cunill

© Bang. Ediciones, 2019

English translation rights arranged through S.B.Rights Agency – Stephanie Barrouillet
Published in English in 2022 by Owlkids Books Inc.
Translation © 2022 Susan Ouriou

Owlkids Books acknowledges the financial support of the Canada Council for the Arts, the
Ontario Arts Council, the Government of Canada through the Canada Book Fund (CBF) and the
Government of Ontario through the Ontario Creates Book Initiative for our publishing activities.

Published in Canada by
Owlkids Books Inc.
1 Eglinton Avenue East
Toronto, ON M4P 3A1

Published in the United States by
Owlkids Books Inc.
1700 Fourth Street
Berkeley, CA 94710

Library and Archives Canada Cataloguing in Publication

Title: Time to go! / written and illustrated by Marta Cunill ; translated by Susan Ouriou.
Other titles: Ya vamos. English
Names: Cunill, Marta, 1986- author, illustrator. | Ouriou, Susan, translator.
Description: Translation of: ¡Ya vamos!
Identifiers: Canadiana 2021037621X | ISBN 9781771475365 (hardcover)
Subjects: LCGFT: Graphic novels. | LCGFT: Picture books.
Classification: LCC PZ7.7.C86 Ti 2022 | DDC j741.5/946—dc23

Library of Congress Control Number: 2021951168

Manufactured in Guangdong Province, Dongguan City, China, in January 2022,
by Toppan Leefung Packaging & Printing (Dongguan) Co., Ltd.

Job #BAYDC104

A   B   C   D   E   F

MIX
Paper from
responsible sources
FSC® C104723

ONTARIO ARTS COUNCIL
CONSEIL DES ARTS DE L'ONTARIO
an Ontario government agency
un organisme du gouvernement de l'Ontario

Canada Council
for the Arts

Conseil des Arts
du Canada

Canada

Publisher of Chirp, Chickadee and OWL
www.owlkidsbooks.com

Owlkids Books is a division of